❄ ❄ ❄ ❄ # Special #3 ❄ ❄ ❄ ❄

THE MYSTERY AT SNOWFLAKE INN

created by
GERTRUDE CHANDLER WARNER

Illustrated by Charles Tang

SCHOLASTIC INC.
New York Toronto London Auckland Sydney

ISBN 0-590-48392-7

12 11 10 9 8 7 6 5 4 3 2 1   4 5 6 7 8 9/9

Printed in the U.S.A.   40

First Scholastic printing, October 1994

Contents

CHAPTER 1

The Old Inn in the Woods

"This is it, Grandfather!" Henry Alden said, examining a map. "Turn left on White Pine Road."

"You're a good guide!" James Alden said.

Being fourteen, Henry knew he should be able to read a map. Still, he was pleased at Grandfather's praise.

Behind Henry were Jessie and Violet, his sisters, and in the back seat, his brother, six-year-old Benny. Next to Benny sat Soo Lee. The little Korean girl was just a year older than Benny and always liked to be with him.

"Soo Lee," Benny said, "I'm glad you could come with us on our winter holiday."

"Yes, indeed," said Grandfather. He knew how much Joe and Alice Alden, their cousins, loved their adopted daughter, and how they hated to be parted from her. But they also wanted Soo Lee to have an old-fashioned New England holiday.

Benny gazed out the back window, his eyes widening as James Alden steered the van onto a narrow road lined with trees on both sides. A sparkling snow blanket covered the hilly land. "I like Vermont!" Benny said, his round face breaking into a smile. "I've never stayed at an old inn before."

Violet, who was ten, returned his smile. "And it's *very* old, Benny. The inn was built when George Washington lived!"

"Wow," Benny whispered. "That's *really* old!"

"Won't it be fun to spend the holidays here?" Jessie asked.

James Alden laughed as the van bumped over a rut. "I thought you children might like to ride in a sleigh pulled by horses, ice skate on a pond, and . . ."

"And hike through the woods," Henry added, folding the map and slipping it into the glove compartment.

They drove past a frozen pond with snow geese clustered nearby.

As they rounded a curve, Jessie gasped at the sight before her eyes. "The inn! How beautiful!" Nestled among the fir trees, the colonial inn looked as white as the snow. White ruffled curtains decorated the many windows and a white sign swung from a post. It read:

SNOWFLAKE INN
1767

"Snowflake Inn," Violet said. "How pretty."

Jessie glanced at Violet. "I hope you brought your paints."

Violet nodded, pleased that her older sister thought she could paint this old inn. Her sketch pad would be the first thing she'd unpack.

Benny pointed to gray smoke drifting up to the blue sky. "Look! Smoke is coming out of the chimney. Do you think there's a fireplace?"

"I'm sure of it!" Grandfather said with a chuckle, as he drove up the circular drive. He stopped before a wide door with a huge wreath tied with a red ribbon.

A patch of color showed through the snow-covered roof. "That red roof reminds me of our red boxcar," Benny said.

"I like the story about where you once lived," Soo Lee said. "You thought your grandfather was mean and you ran away from him." She gave James Alden an impish look.

"We were very wrong," Violet said.

"I'll tell you, though," Henry said, opening the door, "this inn sure looks a lot more comfortable than our boxcar."

"We did make our boxcar cozy, though," Violet said.

"We cooked and cleaned and made it our home," agreed Jessie.

"Yes, you did a good job of living on your

own," Mr. Alden said. "But I'm glad I found you."

"I'm glad, too," Benny said, hopping out of the car. His boots made a crunching sound on the snow.

Soo Lee jumped lightly to the ground behind him.

Benny moved to his grandfather's side. "You're the best grandfather in the whole world."

"Yes, you are," twelve-year-old Jessie said, carrying her suitcase up the brick walk.

"I agree, too," Violet said shyly, following Jessie.

"That makes four of us," Henry said, grabbing two suitcases.

"I like you, also, Mr. . . . " Soo Lee echoed softly.

James threw back his head and laughed. "Please, Soo Lee, call me Grandfather, won't you?"

Soo Lee nodded, giving Mr. Alden a big smile.

Benny took Grandfather's hand, skipping beside the tall, straight-shouldered gentleman. "This is going to be fun!"

Suddenly the door opened and a gray-haired man greeted them. He leaned on a cane, and, although he appeared frail, his voice was steady and strong. "Welcome to Snowflake Inn. You must be the Aldens. I've been waiting for you. I'm Ralph Winston, the owner. Just come this way." His walk was slow because of a slight limp. "After you put your suitcases in the rooms with your names on the doors, I want to show you my inn." He turned and a smile lit his wrinkled face.

Going upstairs, Violet felt the banister wobble under her hand and heard the stairs creak under her boots. The inn looked as if nothing had been done to it for 200 years!

Violet, Jessie, and Soo Lee entered their large room and unpacked. Next door, Henry and Benny hung up their clothes, while down the hall, in his own room, James Alden placed shirts and pants in a drawer.

When everyone was ready, they met Mr. Winston downstairs in the parlor.

"We'll begin our tour of this fine inn right

here," Mr. Winston said. "I've tried to keep it just as it was in 1767."

"I believe it," Jessie murmured, staring up at the beamed ceiling and the peeling wallpaper.

"Dad!" a man of about thirty burst into the room. "The kitchen is a disaster! I've fixed the leaky faucets, but Greta is complaining. She's a good cook and deserves a new stove!" His black eyes flashed, fastening on the older man's face. "Now the sink is cracked. We need a new one!"

"No!" Mr. Winston said firmly. "Leave the sink as it is!"

The young man glared. "This whole place is falling apart!" His black curly hair and short black beard fairly bristled. "I hope it falls down around your ears!"

Benny bit his lip, not daring to breathe. Maybe this vacation wasn't going to be as much fun as he'd thought.

CHAPTER 2

Unfriendly Guests

For a moment the only sound was the ticking of the grandfather clock in the corner. Then Mr. Winston said, "This is my son, Larry."

Larry's features softened and he smiled.

"Meet the Aldens," Ralph Winston said. "Jessie, Violet, Henry, James Alden, Soo Lee, and Benny."

Benny stuck out his hand. "I'm pleased to meet you, Larry Winston."

Larry Winston bent down and graciously shook Benny's hand. "Call me Larry.

Please." He straightened. "You'll have to forgive Dad and me. We're having a constant battle about this inn. I want to modernize it and Dad insists it's fine just the way it is." Larry sighed, looking about. "No television, no phones. I don't mind the TV, but we should have a phone. Snowflake Inn is uncomfortable."

Mr. Winston frowned. "It's not uncomfortable!"

Larry shrugged, holding up his hands. "It's your inn, Dad. I give up." He turned to leave. "I'll see you all later." With his fist, he lightly hit Benny's shoulder. "Maybe we can put together a jigsaw puzzle."

"Yes," Benny said. "I'd like that."

"Well, that's another argument over with," Mr. Winston said, shaking his head and watching as Larry closed the door. "Now, let me tell you about this fireplace." With his cane he pointed out the black marble fireplace, surrounded by white wood and a wooden mantel. The worn colonial sofas, placed on each side of the roaring fire, held needlepoint pillows.

Benny yawned. He hoped Mr. Winston wasn't going to tell them about every antique chair, every lamp, and every table.

They all followed Mr. Winston back to Grandfather's room. Ralph Winston pointed to the large bed. "George Washington stayed overnight at this inn," he paused dramatically, "and he slept in this very bed."

Benny touched a square on the quilt, gazing in awe at the footstool needed to climb into the high bed. "George Washington slept *here?*"

"It's hard to believe, isn't it?" Henry said. "I want to take a picture of this four-poster bed before we leave. If that's okay, Mr. Winston?"

"Call me Ralph." Mr. Winston chuckled, pleased. "Take all the pictures you want."

On the tour, they went through each small, low-ceilinged room with their different shapes. Some were long and narrow. Some were square. As they moved from room to room, the wooden floors creaked.

Benny liked the fireplaces in each bed-

room. Violet admired the old portraits. Henry could have spent the rest of the afternoon in the library. In the dining room, Grandfather examined an antique china cabinet, filled with blue-and-white dishes. Jessie was impressed with the crystal chandelier and the small shade on every electric candle. In the sunny kitchen, Soo Lee pointed to a porcelain rooster. Of everything she'd seen, this was her favorite.

"Hello!" boomed a voice behind them. A woman came bustling in, carrying a bag of onions. "I'm Greta Erickson, the cook."

"And a mighty fine one she is, too!" Ralph Winston said. "She's known for her delicious desserts. Wait until you taste her chocolate cake." He introduced everyone.

Greta winked at the children. "It's a wonder I can cook anything on that ancient stove! It's a wood-burning one!" She shook her head. Soo Lee looked up at Greta. She'd never seen such a tall woman. Thick braids on top of her head made her look even taller.

"You really do love this inn, don't you, Mr. Winston?" Henry asked.

"I sure do. But I'm getting too old to handle it. I'm going to have to retire soon," Ralph Winston said, with an air of regret.

Benny hoped the kitchen was the last room on the tour. He wanted to explore on his own. Ralph, however, held up his hand and said in a low tone, "I have one more place to show you. It's a mysterious nook and has quite a history."

"What is it?" Benny asked in an eager voice.

Ralph, a finger to his lips, hobbled quietly out of the kitchen toward the back stairs. There he stopped.

Puzzled, Benny stared at the brick wall beneath the stairs. "Is this it?" he asked in a disappointed voice.

Ralph Winston chuckled. "That's right, James." And with his cane he pressed against a brick. Slowly, a door opened.

"Wow! A hidden door!" Henry said, peering into the darkness.

"There's no light here, but I've hung a lantern inside." Ralph struck a match and lit the wick, revealing a tiny room.

Jessie edged forward. "A secret room," she marveled, gazing about. She couldn't stand upright because of the slanting stairway overhead.

"What is it for?" Violet questioned, ducking her head and looking inside.

Ralph answered, "During the Revolutionary War, when we fought the British for our freedom, Mr. Whitley, the owner of Snowflake Inn hid Colonial spies in this very nook."

"Wow," Benny said.

"Yessirree," Ralph went on. "He hid Americans who were sneaking secret messages through British lines. The coded messages told the Colonial forces about British troop movements and the size of their regiments. Sometimes, though, these spies were betrayed and had to flee from the Redcoats. If they had been caught, they would have been shot as traitors."

"Redcoats?" Soo Lee asked.

"The British were nicknamed 'Redcoats,'" Henry explained, "because their uniforms had bright red jackets."

"Was George Washington in the war?" Soo Lee asked, her small oval face, framed by short black hair, tilted to one side.

"He was the leading general for the Americans," Violet replied.

Benny stepped inside the tiny niche. "This is a neat hiding place," he said.

Ralph, pleased with himself, smiled. "I thought you might like it. Someday I'll tell you the story of Madge Carson and her daughter." He nodded. "Her daughter, Penelope, was just about your age, Benny."

"Was Madge a spy?" Benny asked, coming out in the open.

"She was one of the best," Ralph responded, "but I'll save that tale for a snowy day. Right now, Greta is serving cake in the dining room." He pressed a brick, and the door swung shut.

Just then, a young woman, dressed in jeans and a jacket, hurried past them.

"Betsy!" Ralph said, "I want you to meet our new guests."

Impatiently, the woman pulled on her gloves. "I'm Betsy Calvert," she said.

"My niece," Ralph said, introducing the Aldens and Soo Lee. "Isn't Betsy a perfect name for someone staying in this old inn?"

"Betsy?" Soo Lee asked.

"Betsy Ross," Ralph said. "She sewed the first American flag."

"Oh, I see," Soo Lee replied. "Thank you."

"I'm pleased to meet you," Betsy said with a frown. She turned to her uncle. "Uncle Ralph, the window in my room is stuck. I can't budge it up or down."

"I'll fix it," Ralph said.

Benny wrinkled his nose, sniffing. He leaned toward Betsy. "You smell good!" he announced.

Violet caught the jasmine scent also, but it was too sweet for her taste.

Betsy stopped and stared at Benny. When she spoke, she said stiffly, "Thank you." Then she brushed by him, and was gone.

Ralph has a very unfriendly niece, thought Jessie. She hoped they wouldn't run into Betsy often.

No sooner had Betsy left when the back

door burst open and a boy and girl about Violet's age dashed through the kitchen and rudely past them.

"That's Davey and Hannah Miller," Ralph said after they'd gone. "They've only been here two days and all they do is complain, or get into trouble. They can't find anything to do, except make mischief, and they want to go home." He smiled at the children. "Maybe now that you've arrived, you can cheer them up."

Violet had her doubts. Poor Mr. Winston. His niece was unfriendly, his son angry and argumentative, and two of his guests wanted to leave. She glanced at Henry. Was he thinking what she was? With some people, no matter how hard you tried, nothing made them happy.

CHAPTER 3

Almost a Sleigh Ride

Before their first dinner at Snowflake Inn, Violet dressed with care, in a striped lavender shirt and purple pants.

"I see you're wearing your favorite colors," Jessie said, as she brushed her long brown hair until it shone.

Violet nodded. "What's your favorite color, Soo Lee?"

"Red," the girl answered instantly.

"Then I think you should have something red," Jessie said, taking a crimson ribbon and tying a bow in Soo Lee's hair.

Pleased, Soo Lee studied herself in the mirror. "Thank you, Jessie."

"We'd better go downstairs," Violet said. "We don't want to be late for dinner."

Mr. Alden met his grandchildren at the head of the stairs and nodded approvingly at their appearance. Benny had slicked back his hair and Henry wore a navy sweater and tan trousers.

Grandfather looked pleased as they entered the dining room.

A pewter tea service, crystal goblets, tall candles, and a blazing fire in the fireplace made the blue room gleam in the soft light.

Larry Winston and Betsy Calvert were seated side by side, and a couple with their two children sat together.

Ralph Winston made certain everyone knew each other. Steven and Rose Miller were the parents of Davey, eight, and Hannah, ten. Henry remembered the Millers' son and daughter by their red hair, which he'd seen earlier. The two had inherited their hair color from Mr. Miller who had an orange fringe around his bald head.

Jessie smiled at the Miller children, and hoped they'd join in the fun at the inn. But by their angry expressions, she wasn't sure they'd want to.

Mr. Winston rang a small silver bell, and Greta entered with a covered bowl.

With a flourish the cook lifted off the lid. "Beef stew!" she crowed. "The meat finally got done. No thanks to that old stove!"

"It smells delicious," Violet said, placing her napkin in her lap.

"And looks yummy," Benny added, rubbing his stomach. "I'm hungry!"

"When aren't you hungry?" Henry said with a chuckle.

Soo Lee passed a platter to Betsy. "Would you like some carrots, Betsy Ross?" she asked.

Davey's freckled face broke into a wide grin, and Hannah stifled a giggle.

"It's not Betsy Ross!" Betsy corrected irritably. "It's Betsy Calvert!"

"I'm sorry," Soo Lee apologized. Her lower lip trembled.

"It's all right," Jessie said. "Look, here are some pickled apples." She put one on Soo Lee's plate. "You'll like them."

Soo Lee returned her smile. Jessie made everything all right again.

Mr. Miller put down his fork and said in a cheerful voice, "Tomorrow you'll have a good time, Davey. Do you know the surprise that's planned?"

Davey shrugged. "I don't care. I just wish we weren't here!"

Rose Miller put on a smile. "Wouldn't you like to ride in a horse-drawn sleigh?"

Davey shrugged. "I guess so."

Hannah played with her potatoes. "Maybe a sleigh ride would be okay, but it's just so boring here."

"You can say that again!" Davey said. "Why couldn't we have gone to an amusement park instead?"

"We thought you'd like an old-fashioned holiday," her mother said.

"Snowflake Inn is such an historic place!" Steven Miller said. "Isn't it exciting that

George Washington stayed here?"

Unimpressed, Davey took a deep breath, gazing at the ceiling.

"I think a sleigh ride will be fun," Benny piped up. "We can sing as we go."

Throwing down his napkin, Davey said, "I'm going to my room."

Rose bit her lip. "All right, dear, but don't you want a piece of Greta's chocolate cake?"

"No," Davey said, standing.

It was too bad Davey was so unhappy, Violet thought. She wondered how they could cheer him up. She wished Hannah would be her friend. She was just her age. But how could you make friends with someone so grouchy?

When dinner was finished, Ralph Winston challenged Grandfather to a chess game.

Larry brought out a jigsaw puzzle, and the Alden children settled around a table before the fireplace. Violet beckoned to Hannah, pointing to an empty chair beside her.

Slowly Hannah sat down, and for a while seemed to enjoy herself. But when Davey called to her from the head of the stairs, she quickly leaped up, moving to the doorway.

"Let's meet in the morning at the stable for the sleigh ride," Violet called.

Hannah paused. "Is ten o'clock okay?"

Violet said, "That's fine. We'll be there."

Maybe Hannah and Davey just needed a few friends their own age, Violet thought.

Soon Benny's eyelids grew heavy and his head drooped forward.

Jessie stretched. She was tired, too. It had been a long day. The children said good night to Larry, Ralph, and Grandfather, and went to bed.

In the morning, after a breakfast of sausages and Greta's Swedish pancakes with delicious Vermont maple syrup, the children put on their jackets, mittens, and knit caps.

"I can't wait!" Benny said. "Won't a ride in the snow be fun?"

"It's not ten o'clock yet, but we can go out and wait for the others," Jessie said.

"Let's go," Benny said impatiently, tugging at Henry's jacket.

Henry laughed, lifting Benny up on his shoulders. "We're off on a sleigh ride!"

When the Aldens arrived at the stable, Hannah and Davey were already waiting.

They certainly got here early, Jessie thought.

Suddenly Larry hurried out from the stable. "The horses!" he exclaimed. "The horses are missing!"

Benny's mouth dropped open. "The horses are *gone?* Did they run away?"

"Someone left the stall door open and let them out!" Larry said grimly.

"You mean a person deliberately let the horses go free?" Henry asked with a frown.

Violet glanced at Hannah and Davey and was puzzled to see that they didn't look at all surprised. It was almost as if they'd known all along the horses were gone. "Let's go in, Hannah," Davey said as he got to his feet. "I knew something would happen to ruin the day!"

Jessie stared after the Millers as they walked slowly up the path. Who would have let the horses out on purpose. And why?

CHAPTER 4

Missing Horses!

Mystified, Larry Winston rubbed his neatly trimmed beard. "I can't figure out why anyone would do this."

"Will the horses come back?" Benny asked in a worried tone. "I hope they're not hurt."

"I'm certain Dobbin and Robin are fine," Larry said. He noticed all the anxious expressions. "It's all right. I have a good idea where the horses probably went."

"Not very far, I hope," Henry said.

"No, not far at all," Larry answered. "Just over at Brian McDowell's farm. About two miles from here on Apple Tree Road." He climbed into his jeep. "Brian will bring them back in his horse trailer." He waved. "I'll be back soon." He turned on the engine and started down the lane.

"Let's look around and see if any clues have been left," Jessie said.

"Clues?" Soo Lee questioned.

"Something that the person who freed the horses left behind," Jessie explained.

Violet and Jessie searched the stable, but they found nothing.

Henry and Soo Lee checked the ground around the barn.

Benny found nothing, too.

"Henry," Soo Lee said, "there are footprints here in the fresh snow."

Henry moved to her side.

Benny hurried over to look, also. "What a lot of footprints!"

"Yes," Henry replied. "And I don't think Larry made them all."

"See," Soo Lee said, stooping. "There's a picture in each footprint."

Henry chuckled. "There is a picture, Soo

Lee, but it's called a pattern or design." He sat on his haunches, studying the footprints. "Inside the heel is a pattern like a small horseshoe."

"I think it's shaped like a wishbone," Benny said, leaning over, hands on his knees.

When the girls came out of the stable, Benny showed them what Soo Lee had discovered.

"You've found a wonderful clue, Soo Lee," Violet said, squeezing the little girl's hand. "You'll make a good detective."

Soo Lee beamed. "Thank you."

"Now we need to keep a sharp lookout for whoever wears boots with heels like that," Jessie said.

"We're all dressed in our warm clothes," Henry said. "Let's not go in. What can we do outdoors?"

"We can play tag," Jessie suggested.

"Or Fox and Geese," Benny added. "That's like tag."

"Yes," Violet said. "You need snow to form a big circle." Violet pointed to a large patch of untrampled snow. "There's the perfect place."

"Oh, good," Soo Lee said, clapping her hands. "This will be fun. We have snow in Korea, but I've never played Fox and Geese."

"I'll run in and get Davey and Hannah," Benny offered. "I'll bet they'd like to play."

"Okay, Benny," Henry said, although he doubted that the Miller children would join in.

But Henry's eyes widened when Benny came out with Davey and Hannah.

First, the children dashed around, forming a big circle by trampling down the snow. Then they made paths up to the center, which was the safe zone. When the circle was completed it resembled a big wheel with spokes.

Jessie was "It," and chased first Soo Lee, then Benny, then Violet, then Henry, then Davey, and finally Hannah. They were the "geese," and they always seemed to land in the safe center, no matter how fast Jessie ran.

At last Jessie tagged Henry. Now, he became "It." For an hour the children zigged and zagged, trying not to be caught.

After Henry tagged Violet, she was "It," and chased after Davey. Davey yelled as he dashed around the circle. Suddenly, the young boy slipped and fell. Violet rushed to help him to his feet. She lifted him and brushed snow from his ski jacket.

Hurrying over to aid her brother, Hannah laughed as she dusted snow from Davey's cap and hair. "You're covered from head to foot."

Davey pushed the girls away. "I'm tired of this silly old game. I'm not playing anymore!" A frown crossed his round face which was covered with even more freckles than his sister's. He stepped out of the circle.

"I think it's time for hot chocolate," Jessie said, trying to soothe Davey's feelings.

"Yes! Yes!" Benny agreed, stamping his feet to keep warm. "I'm cold. Hot chocolate in my pink cup will taste good."

"Your poor chipped cup from our boxcar days," Violet said. "I can't believe it's not broken into a hundred pieces."

"I take good care of it," Benny said. "I

wouldn't want to break my favorite cup."

"I know, Benny," Henry said, throwing his arm around Benny's shoulders. "Let's go up to the inn." He looked back. "Coming, Davey?"

"I guess so," the little boy answered, kicking at the snow.

In the cozy kitchen, Greta filled cups with hot chocolate. She took the tray of cups and a plate of cookies into the living room and put them on a low oak table before the fireplace.

Hannah, Davey, and Violet sat on the sofa, while Henry and Jessie made themselves comfortable in two armchairs on each side of the fire. Benny and Soo Lee sat crosslegged before the yellow flames.

"Hmmm," Benny said, sipping his chocolate, "this is a nice place." He glanced at Davey. "Don't you think so, Davey?"

"It's okay," Davey said, "but it's very different from where we live!"

Hannah gave a nod of agreement.

"Where are you from?" Violet asked politely.

"Boston!" Davey replied.

"That's a big place!" Benny said.

"It's one of the best cities in the world," Hannah said, smiling.

"Outside of Greenfield, Massachusetts," Benny said.

"There's always something to do in Boston!" Davey said.

"I'm sure Boston is fun," Benny said. "But Vermont is fun, too!"

Henry said with a grin, "Benny, no matter where we go, you find something to like."

"I like it here, too," Soo Lee said, a smile brightening her face.

Violet placed the empty cups on the tray and asked, "Who wants to play a game of Monopoly?"

Benny's arm shot straight up. "Me, me!"

Soo Lee giggled, holding up her arm. "Me, me."

"I'll get the board," Jessie said.

"I wonder where Grandfather is," Henry said. "He promised to play a game of chess with me." He headed for the den. "See you later."

Hannah dealt out the play money and the game began.

By the time the game had a winner, with Jessie owning most of the property and money, it was almost lunchtime.

Benny jumped up when he heard the honking of a horn. "Larry's back with the horses!"

"Let's go outside and meet him," Violet said.

Hastily, the children slipped into their jackets, and ran outside.

Larry waved, climbing out of his jeep.

Benny peered down the road and all around, but he didn't see any horses. "Where are Dobbin and Robin?" he asked.

Where are the horses? Violet wondered. Had Larry been wrong about where the horses had gone? She took a breath, feeling scared. As she gazed about at the long faces, she knew she wasn't the only one. Where were the missing horses? Was something wrong?

CHAPTER 5

More Trouble at Snowflake Inn

"Where are the horses?" Benny asked as Larry Winston approached them.

"They're not lost," Larry reassured him. "Dobbin and Robin were right where I said they'd be — in Brian McDowell's meadow. But before Brian can load the horses, he needs to round up a cow that jumped the fence. So instead of going on a sleigh ride now, how would you like to go tonight in the moonlight?"

Benny smiled. "Great!"

"How about it, kids? Does a moonlight ride sound okay?" Larry asked.

"Yes!" everyone chorused. Davey and Hannah nodded, but they didn't look very excited.

On the back porch, Greta jangled a big bell.

"Lunch! We're coming, Greta!" Larry called. "I'm starved. How about you, Davey?" He messed up Davey's red hair.

Davey nodded. "I could eat."

"The cold sure gave me an appetite," Henry said, following Larry inside.

"Me, too," Benny agreed.

Soon, a delicious lunch of chili, corn bread, salad, and coconut cream pie was devoured. Greta chuckled to see how fast her food disappeared.

After eating, Soo Lee leaned back in her chair, closing her eyes. "I ate a lot."

"How about a nap?" Violet asked.

Soo Lee rubbed her eyes, yawning. "Yes, I'm sleepy!"

So Soo Lee curled up on the sofa, Jessie and Hannah played checkers, Davey and

Benny worked a new jigsaw puzzle, Henry read, and Violet sketched the tall canopy bed and fireplace in her bedroom.

After an hour, Ralph Winston rounded everyone up. "Come into the den," he said, pointing to the window. "Do you see what I see?"

"It's snowing!" Benny said.

Big flakes drifted to the ground. "How beautiful!" Violet said.

"You promised you'd tell us the story of Madge Carson and Penelope on a snowy day," Jessie said. "Will you, Mr. Winston?"

"Ralph," he corrected. "Call me Ralph." He limped toward the den. "Yes, telling Madge's story is exactly what I had in mind. That's why I wanted all of you together.

"Madge Carson and her little girl, Penelope, lived in Trenton, New Jersey," Ralph began, sinking into an easy chair by the window as the children gathered around, sitting cross-legged at his feet. "Across the Delaware River from them was George Washington's army at Valley Forge."

"On Christmas Eve," he went on, "a few

British and paid German soldiers, called Hessians, were left to guard Trenton. Now, the troops planned a party and ordered Madge to bring them a dozen chickens. She knew that while the enemy partied it would be a perfect time for a surprise attack. Madge rowed across the icy river and told George Washington."

"Did General Washington fight the Hessians?" Violet asked.

"You bet he did! Washington and his soldiers crossed the river and trounced the astonished Hessians."

Betsy poked her head in. "I see you're still retelling Madge Carson's story." A tight little smile crossed her face. "No wonder. You've got a captive audience!"

"Hi, Betsy," Ralph said. "Want to join us?"

The slim young woman, dressed in boots, riding pants, and a plaid fitted jacket, held up her hand. "No, thank you. I came because of the leak in my bedroom ceiling. This new snow could crack the plaster."

"Find Larry. He'll fix it," Ralph said,

wrinkling his brow. "I'm busy."

"Hmmmf! If it was up to Larry he'd re-plaster — and repaint — all these old walls," Betsy said. She left, shaking her head.

"Now, where was I?" The old man tugged on his ear.

"What happened to Madge Carson?" Henry asked.

"When the Redcoats discovered Madge was missing, they knew she had spied on them," Ralph said.

"Redcoats were British soliders," Soo Lee announced, remembering what Henry had told her.

"Good for you!" Henry said, smiling at her.

"Madge dared not go home, so she ran into the woods. There, she hid, sheltering her little daughter against the cold."

"Poor Madge," Jessie said.

"Poor Penelope," Violet echoed.

"Madge avoided capture because she knew woodland trails and the river," Ralph con-tinued. "Snow and cold made it hard to travel, especially with a small child. Finally, they arrived at Bennington, in what is now Vermont. Madge and Penelope were hid by the Ross family, original owners of Snow-flake Inn."

"Did Madge and Penelope hide in the secret room?" Benny asked, his eyes round.

"When British troops arrived to search the inn, that's exactly where they hid," Ralph answered.

"I'll bet Penelope was scared," Soo Lee said in a small voice.

"They were both afraid," Ralph said, "but, with help, they managed to escape to Maine."

"That was an exciting story," Hannah said, her pretty face breaking into a smile.

"And to think it was a true one!" Henry said.

"Was Madge Carson the only one who hid in the secret room?" Davey asked.

"No, she wasn't," Ralph said. "During the Civil War several spies hid here. And Snow-flake Inn hid slaves on the Underground Railroad."

"Underground Railroad?" Soo Lee asked,

"Did a train run under the ground?"

"No, no," answered Jessie, smiling. "In the Civil War, slaves who escaped from their owners were hidden by sympathetic people. The slaves were moved secretly from one house to another, all the way to Canada. This became known as the Underground Railroad."

"Oh, I see," Soo Lee said.

Later, when the sky darkened, Benny gazed out the window. "Is it time for our sleigh ride?" he asked impatiently.

"In a few hours," replied Jessie.

All at once, Greta stormed into the room, jabbing the air with a wooden spoon. "The stove won't work!" she said angrily, one hand planted on a hip. "If the stove doesn't work, neither do I!"

Oh, no, Henry thought. The horses are missing, the sink is cracked, the plaster's coming down, and now the stove is broken! What next?

CHAPTER 6

A Moonlight Sleigh Ride

Later that night, Benny was the first one ready to go on the sleigh ride. When he entered the den dressed in his warm jacket, cap, and mittens, Grandfather looked up from his book. "I see you're eager to go, Benny."

"Yes," Benny replied. "I can't wait, Grandfather. Why don't you come along on our sleigh ride?"

James Alden chuckled. "Thanks, Benny, but I'm comfortable sitting here by the fire. You go ahead and have a good time!"

"Oh, I will." Benny gave him a big smile. "We'll have a great time!" With a wave, he dashed off to join the others, who were waiting by the front door.

Ralph Winston clapped Davey on the back. "I'll hear all about your ride in the morning. Have fun, children!"

"Wouldn't you like to come along?" Violet asked.

Ralph shook his head. "No," he replied. "I'm going to turn in early."

"Then we'll see you tomorrow," Jessie said, opening the door. She was glad Ralph was going to bed. He worked hard and looked very frail. Clearly, he wasn't well and needed rest.

"Hurry up, Davey!" Benny yelled. "I'll race you to the stable."

The two boys tore down the path, and arrived breathless just as Larry hitched the horses to the sleigh. Dobbin and Robin snorted and stamped. As Larry fastened bells to the bridles, the horses blew out their breaths in white puffs.

While the boys clambered aboard, Jessie,

Violet, and Hannah petted the horses. Noticing the snow underfoot, Jessie said to Violet, "These are Larry's footprints!"

In the brightness of the yard light, Violet stooped, peering at the ground. "Yes, Larry's boot leaves an imprint of a horseshoe in the heel. But I can't believe Larry would have let the horses out. He's too nice."

"Let's keep our eyes open. Maybe someone else has the same heel design," Jessie suggested.

"Yes, I'm sure it's a popular pattern," Violet said. Yet, she remembered Larry's fight with his dad.

"Come on, everybody," Larry said, smiling, "into the sleigh!"

Once the children were settled on the side benches, Larry lightly touched the horses with the reins, and they pranced forward.

Violet said, "What fun!" She gazed about at the snow-covered fir trees. Big flakes continued to fall softly over everyone.

Rounding a curve, bells tinkled and horse hooves clip-clopped in the silent night.

"It's a fairyland," Henry said.

All at once Benny gave a gleeful yelp. He began to sing. "Jingle Bells, jingle bells, jingle all the way." Laughing, everyone else sang, too. "Oh, what fun it is to ride in a one-horse open sleigh!"

They sang and laughed for mile after snowy mile.

After an hour, Larry headed back to Snowflake Inn. When they'd almost reached the stable, Larry slowed and almost stopped.

"What's wrong?" Davey asked.

Larry chuckled. "Do you see what I see?"

Jessie craned her neck. A fat porcupine waddled across the road.

"I've never seen a porcupine before," Davey said, watching until the animal had disappeared into the woods.

"I have," Benny said proudly. "Once we helped a friend straighten out his mixed-up zoo."

Davey's eyes widened, impressed. "You did?"

Back at the inn, the children chattered and laughed all the way inside where they removed their jackets.

"Hi," Betsy called. "Did you have fun?"

"Yes, lots of fun," Violet said.

Hannah and Davey went upstairs, and the Aldens entered the living room.

Betsy, curled up in an easy chair with her stocking feet under her, put down her magazine. She'd placed her boots by the footstool. One boot had toppled over.

Henry stared at the boot. A horseshoe, outlined in the heel of the boot, could be seen clearly.

Betsy rose and stretched, running her hand through her blonde hair. "Hi, Cousin," she said to Larry, who came into the room.

"Hi, Betsy," Larry said, his lips pressed together. He held a piece of paper.

"How about a cup of coffee?" Betsy asked, picking up her boots.

"I could use one," Larry admitted. "Dad left me a note, asking me to fix the rusty pipe in my bathroom. That could take all night!" As he and Betsy left the room, Larry said, "I don't see why he won't just put in completely new plumbing! This old inn isn't going to last long at this rate! Someone is going to have to do something."

Betsy laughed. "You'll never change Uncle Ralph!"

Once Larry and Betsy were in the kitchen, Henry, leaning against the fireplace mantel, said, "Did anyone else notice Betsy's boot?"

"No, why?" Jessie asked.

"The heel had a horseshoe pattern," he replied.

Violet said, "Well, we know Larry's boots also have that same horseshoe design."

"Yes, we saw it again tonight in the snow," Jessie said.

"Larry acts like this is *his* inn," Henry said. "He wants to change all kinds of things around here." He dropped down onto the footstool.

Henry said, "Betsy might want Snowflake Inn for herself, too!"

"Yes," Jessie agreed. "She's Ralph's niece. He might let her take over the inn."

Yes, Jessie thought, both Betsy and Larry stood a good chance to inherit the inn. Were they trying to make so much trouble that Ralph would give up the inn now?

CHAPTER 7

Fire and Smoke

In the morning, after a hearty breakfast, the Aldens dressed to go ice skating. Davey and Hannah stood in the hallway. Henry noticed some soot on Hannah's sweater. "What happened?" he asked.

"Oh, Davey and I were just playing around near the fireplace and I fell down," Hannah explained.

"Would you like to come skating with us?" Violet asked.

"We didn't bring our ice skates," Davey said in a glum tone.

"I know what we'll do!" Benny said with a big smile, "I'll skate a while and then you can borrow my ice skates, Davey."

"That's a good idea, Benny," Jessie said. "We'll take turns."

"Hannah, my skates will fit you," Violet said. "We'll miss you if you don't come along."

"You will?" Hannah said in surprise.

"Yes, we will," Soo Lee said, giving them a little smile.

Pleased, Davey and Hannah hurried to get their jackets.

"Did I hear a pair of ice skates were needed?" Larry asked, coming into the room. His hair was messy, dark circles underlined his eyes, and his denim shirt was dirty. "Davey, you can use my old pair. I discovered them in the basement." He added angrily, "Where I've been all night, patching a crack in the boiler. I'm the number one repairman around here!"

His old friendly smile returned. "So, lucky for you, Davey, I ran across the ice skates I owned when I was your age." He turned as

Ralph entered the room. "Oh, good morning, Dad."

"Good morning, everyone," Ralph answered. "Is the boiler fixed, Larry?"

"I think it might last another week or so," Larry said in a cool tone.

Ralph shook his head. "I suppose I'd better order a new one."

"Of course, you should!" Larry snapped. "If the boiler breaks and floods the basement we'll have a real mess on our hands!" He turned and headed for the basement.

Ralph glanced at the children, then went over to a chair, sank down wearily, and rubbed his forehead.

Ralph looked ready to give up on Snowflake Inn, Henry thought. Maybe that was why he didn't seem in a rush to order a new boiler.

When Larry returned, he handed Davey his skates.

On the way to the pond, Violet walked beside Hannah. "Don't worry, Hannah. You can wear my skates most of the time. I want to sketch the ice skaters."

"Thanks," said Hannah. "That's really nice of you."

Arriving at the pond, the children laced up their ice skates. Violet sat on the side sketching the pond.

Jessie skimmed onto the ice, doing a spin or two.

"Jessie's like a real ice skater!" Davey said.

"She sure is!" Benny replied. "Jessie can skate backward, go fast, and do spins!"

"Where did she learn to skate so fancy?" Hannah asked, clearly admiring Jessie's grace and agility.

"From a professional ice skater," Henry explained, standing up. "You see, an ice skating troupe performed in Greenfield. We became friends with them."

"Alex was one of the stars and a wonderful skater," Violet added. "She taught Jessie different moves. She said Jessie was a natural."

Benny tottered out on the ice, then unsteadily skated to the other side of the small pond. "Coming, Davey?" he shouted.

Davey pulled his cap down over his ears and skated to Benny's side.

Jessie glided around the edge of the pond, then did a perfect pirouette in the center.

"Beautiful, Jessie," Violet called. "Do that again! I want to sketch you."

Soo Lee skated to Henry, and grabbed his hand. Henry laughed, motioning Hannah to join them. Soon all the skaters formed a line, hanging on to each other's waists. With Henry as the leader they zoomed around the pond. When the wind blew off Benny's cap, he laughed with glee.

Soon Hannah skated to the edge of the pond. "Violet, it's your turn to skate."

Shaking her hand, Violet said, "No, thanks, I want to finish this drawing."

So for the rest of the morning Hannah and the others skated, often stopping to pose for Violet.

"Hey!" Larry yelled as he arrived, standing up in the sleigh pulled by Robin and Dobbin, "how about a ride back to the inn? Greta has hot apple cider waiting for you!"

Eagerly the children removed their skates and climbed aboard the sleigh. They were ready for the warm inn and a hot drink.

Ralph, looking rested and happier, said as they arrived, "How about a fire, children?"

"Oh, could we?" Benny asked, his face shining.

"You bet!" Ralph answered. He bent down to Soo Lee. "Would you like a fire?"

"Yes, I would," Soo Lee said, looking up at Ralph with big, dark eyes.

Ralph chuckled, and with creaky knees, he kneeled on the hearth of the brick fireplace. "I've ordered a new boiler," he said matter-of-factly, "so nothing else should go wrong." He lit a match to the papers beneath the logs, and flames shot up the chimney.

In a short time smoke filled the room.

Jessie coughed and Violet held her hand over her nose and mouth. Tears welled up in Benny's eyes. "What's wrong with the fire?" he asked in a choked voice.

Ralph's eyes watered, too, as he used the poker to push aside the wood. Pouring water over the flames, he tried to extinguish the fire. Waving to the children and holding a handkerchief over his face, he wheezed,

"Children, go into the kitchen."

As the children left the room with their eyes watering, they met Larry who immediately took in the situation. He rushed to his father's side and helped put out the smouldering embers.

In the kitchen, Henry opened a window and Hannah opened the back door. The children huddled around the kitchen table. Benny sighed. They were having such a good time, and then this had to happen.

Larry, his face streaked with soot, entered the kitchen. "The fire's out!" he announced.

"What caused the smoke?" Violet questioned.

"Would you believe the chimney had been stuffed with rags and an old coat?" Larry said. "The smoke couldn't escape."

"Who would want to suffocate us?" Violet asked.

"I wish I knew," Larry said, pressing his lips together.

Henry recalled that Larry's clothes had been all dirty earlier. Maybe the dirt wasn't just from fixing the boiler. Then again, Hannah's sweater had been sooty. Could she and Davey be to blame?

Grandfather and Betsy came in the back door. "What has happened to you?" Grandfather asked. "You all look as if you've been crying!"

"We have!" Benny said in a loud voice. "But we're okay now."

"Grandfather, the chimney was stopped up," explained Jessie. "The den filled with smoke!"

"Is everything all right now?" Mr. Alden asked with concern, resting a hand on Henry's shoulder.

"Yes, it's fine now," Larry said. "We let plenty of fresh air in."

"Oh, dear," Betsy wailed. "I feel awful. Here I was out horseback riding, breathing in cold winter air."

Jessie gave Betsy a look. She wondered if Betsy really felt as badly as she said she did.

CHAPTER 8

Rustlings in the Night

On the fourth day of the Alden vacation, Henry rose early to help Larry clean the stable and curry the horses. He loved horses and was glad he could be around them.

On the way to the stable, Henry asked Larry, "Do you have any idea who would clog the chimney?" Secretly, he wondered if it might be Larry himself. If Larry couldn't get his way and modernize the inn, maybe he was deliberately trying to mess things up.

"I haven't a clue," Larry answered. "But

I know one thing! That coat didn't get up the chimney by itself!" He gave Henry a sideways look. "It could be those kids, Davey and Hannah. They're so bored, they might do anything for a little excitement."

Larry handed Henry an apple. "Give this treat to Dobbin. He'll be your friend for life."

Entering the stable, Henry sniffed the smell of hay and horses. What a pleasing odor — much better than Betsy's jasmine perfume!

Larry and Henry worked well together. The stalls were cleaned and the horses brushed before breakfast.

At the breakfast table, Violet asked, "Where is Grandfather?"

"He went along with Dad and Mr. and Mrs. Miller, to the antiques fair in town," Larry said.

"I wonder what Greta cooked today," Benny said, licking his lips.

Greta, carrying a platter of pancakes and bacon, said, "Well, Benny, does this answer your question?"

"Oh, boy! Pancakes!" Benny said. He rubbed his stomach. "I love pancakes!"

Soon, the heaping platter was empty.

"Now, what can we do?" Davey asked in a bored tone.

Betsy entered, and reached across the table, taking a banana from the fruit bowl in the center.

Jessie, glancing about, said, "You know, this old inn needs holiday spirit!"

"I know," Violet said. "The wreath on the front door is all the decoration there is."

"We can put up pine boughs!" Jessie suggested.

"And string popcorn," Henry added.

"Why don't you children come into town with me this afternoon," Greta said. "Mr. Winston has given me money for groceries and other things. You children can buy some decorations and spruce up Snowflake!"

"Yes!" Soo Lee said. "We'll make the inn pretty."

"Then it's settled," Greta said, her arms crossed. "After lunch we go to town."

Betsy wrinkled her nose in disgust. "No

matter how hard you try, you can't make this place attractive."

"Wait and see," Violet said with a smile. Why, she wondered, was Betsy always so sour wherever the inn was concerned?

Benny to the hall, lifting his jacket off a peg. "I'm collecting pinecones," he announced.

"Good idea! Let's go for a hike in the woods and as we walk we'll gather pinecones and holly," Jessie said, tying a wool scarf around her neck.

"Okay," Davey said half-heartedly. "At least it's *something* to do!"

"I'm ready," Henry said, putting on ear-muffs, and opening the door.

The children trudged through the snow and into the pine woods. Benny dashed ahead, scooping up snow and letting it drift over his face. "I love winter!" he shouted, his words echoing through the trees.

"Look!" Jessie called, plowing through a drift to a bush. "Holly bushes!"

Hannah, who had brought a pail, joined her. Soon everyone was gathering bunches

of holly and pinecones. Henry broke off a few pine boughs for the mantel in the den.

The morning flew by. When the children returned to Snowflake Inn, they carried a bucketful of pinecones and armfuls of fir branches and holly.

Later, after lunch, Greta drove them to town in the station wagon, and pulled up before a large discount store. The children spilled out, eager to buy decorations while Greta went on to the grocery store.

Going down the aisles of the store the children located holiday items. Jessie picked out red and green candles, and Benny and Soo Lee selected candy canes. Hannah and Violet chose crimson and green ribbons, Davey picked out some tinsel, and Henry found a large wreath.

Back at the inn, the children began to decorate. Jessie popped corn, then with Davey's help, strung it on a gold cord along with some cranberries Greta had bought. Violet and Hannah framed the front door with the popcorn and cranberry strings. Henry arranged pine boughs and red candles in the middle of the dining-room table. The large wreath was hung above the fireplace in the den by Jessie. Soo Lee and Benny strewed holly and pinecones on the mantel.

"Look what I've got, Benny," Henry said, holding up a sprig of mistletoe.

Benny's eyes grew big. "Where does that go?"

"Above the door going into the den," Henry answered, standing on a chair and fastening the mistletoe to the door beam.

"What's it for?" Benny wanted to know.

"Anyone standing under this gets a kiss."

Benny covered his mouth with his hand, giggling. "That's mushy stuff. You won't catch me under any old mistletoe!"

"Dinner!" Greta called.

"We need to finish," Benny replied.

"After you've eaten, you can go back to work," Greta said.

So after dinner the decorating continued. For an hour the children bustled from one room to another. When they were done, and the candles were lit and a cozy fire burned in the fireplace, the children stood back and admired their work. Snowflake Inn looked as warm and festive as the children felt.

When Grandfather and the others returned from the fair, their *ohs* and *ahs* made the children happy. They had worked hard, and were pleased that their holiday trimmings were appreciated.

That night, snuggled beneath the covers, Violet fell sound asleep. But around midnight, she awakened, hearing a strange rustling. "Jessie," she whispered, not wanting to wake Soo Lee.

"Ummmm," Jessie murmured, rolling over.

The rustling noise became louder.

Violet's heart thumped and she could hardly breathe. "Jessie!" she urgently whispered, shaking her. "Listen! Someone's in our room!"

CHAPTER 9

Greta Quits!

Jessie awoke with a start. "What's wrong, Violet?"

"Shhh, listen," Violet answered.

Jessie tilted her head. Sure enough, the sound of rustling papers came from the corner. Quietly, Jessie threw back the covers and switched on the desk lamp. Violet, sticking close to her side, followed.

"No one's here," Jessie said, peering around the room.

"Shall we check the closet?" Violet questioned.

Jessie shook her head. Putting a finger to her lips, she advanced on the wastebasket. All was silent. Suddenly, papers stirred in the wastebasket. Jessie pointed downward.

"What's in there?" Soo Lee said, rubbing her eyes and peeping inside the basket.

In her bare feet, Jessie crept toward the corner, reaching for her umbrella.

Violet took a lamp and held it close to the basket, while Jessie poked about in the papers.

"Squeak! Squeak!"

Jessie glanced back at Violet and smiled.

Violet bent nearer. She smiled, too. "Why, it's a sweet little field mouse."

Jessie scooped up the furry mouse, cupping it in her hands. "Let's put it outside so it will find its way back to its nest."

Violet opened the bedroom door and the three girls tiptoed downstairs.

"How would a field mouse find its way upstairs and into our wastebasket?" Violet said in a puzzled tone. "It seems more likely it would have been poking around in the kitchen, where there's food."

"You're right," Jessie answered. "Maybe someone deliberately put the mouse in our room to scare us."

Opening the front door, Violet felt cold air rush over her. Jessie gently placed the mouse on the doormat.

With a last squeak, the mouse dashed toward freedom and home.

"I heard the front door open," Henry said, coming down the steps, trailed by a sleepy Benny.

"We opened the door for a mouse," Jessie replied.

"A real mouse?" Benny asked, becoming wide awake.

"A real mouse," Violet replied with a smile. Then she related the story of the mouse in the wastebasket.

"I wish it had been in our wastebasket," Benny said, a wistful look on his face. Then he brightened. "Know what? I'm hungry."

"What a surprise," Henry said.

"How about a snack?" Jessie said.

"But Greta keeps the kitchen locked," Soo Lee said.

"Greta left a jar of cookies in the den," Violet suddenly remembered.

"Ummmm, yes," Benny said eagerly, hurrying into the den.

Sitting on the sofa in front of the cold fireplace, Violet said, "We think somebody put the mouse in our room."

"Why would someone do that?" Benny asked.

"Maybe to frighten us," Jessie said, pausing as she reached for a cookie. "Maybe someone wants us out of here for some reason."

Benny took a big bite of his chocolate chip cookie. "A little mouse isn't going to make us leave!"

Chuckling, Henry replied, "That's right, Benny. Some people, though, are afraid of mice and might have screamed." He glanced fondly at his sisters. "Whoever it was didn't know Violet and Jessie."

"A lot of things are happening that shouldn't be happening." Jessie rested her chin on her hand, thinking, "Remember the soot on Hannah's sweater the morning the chimney was clogged? Maybe Hannah and Davey left the mouse as a prank."

"Both Larry and Betsy had a horseshoe pattern — we saw it on their boot heels," Violet pointed out. "One of them might want to get the guests to leave."

"Maybe both of them," Henry said. "They could be in this together."

"I don't know," Jessie said. "My head is spinning."

"Let's go to bed," Violet said. "Tomorrow we'll see things in a clearer light."

The Aldens slept soundly that night and were in a good mood until they got downstairs. From the kitchen came the banging of pots and pans. All at once, Greta flung open the door. "The stove is broken again! And someone pulled out the refrigerator plug and ice cream has melted all over!"

"Not more troubles," Henry said.

"Yes, *more*," Greta replied. "And I keep the kitchen door locked at night, so I don't know how anyone got in, either."

"I'll repair the stove," Ralph soothed. "Don't worry, Greta."

"I'm not waiting!" Greta shouted, removing her apron and throwing it on a chair. "I quit!"

"Now, Greta," Ralph began, "we — "

But before he could finish his sentence, Greta stalked to the closet and struggled into her coat. Storming out, she slammed the door after her.

"Greta's gone," Ralph muttered, dropping into a chair. His face was gray with disappointment. "Since the stove isn't working, I'm afraid there won't be any hot breakfast. Day after tomorrow we were to have our big holiday dinner. Looks like you were right, Larry. I should modernize the inn." He shook his head. "Everything is going wrong!" He glanced up with sad eyes, looking at the Millers and James Alden. "I'll refund your money."

The stunned children stared at Ralph. Benny grabbed Grandfather's hand. Was their vacation at Snowflake Inn over so soon?

CHAPTER 10

Broken Glass

James Alden looked at the sad faces of his grandchildren, then turned to Ralph Winston and said, "We're staying!"

The Aldens shouted, "Hooray!"

"We'll stay, too," Mrs. Miller said, looking at her husband who nodded in agreement.

"Wonderful," Ralph said. "But how can we cook without a stove?"

"I have an idea," Grandfather said. "Will you allow me to buy a new stove?"

"That's very kind of you." Ralph sighed.

"But a new stove will ruin the look of our colonial kitchen."

Grandfather said, "Trust me, Ralph. I have an idea. Just tell me where I can find an appliance store."

"But who will cook our big dinner?" Ralph questioned.

"We will!" the Aldens chorused.

"And maybe Davey and Hannah can help," Violet suggested.

"But I don't know how to cook," Davey protested.

"Neither do I," Hannah said.

"Don't worry," Henry said. "You can cut up onions and celery, can't you?"

"I guess so," Davey replied.

Hannah brightened. "We'll help."

"Then that's settled," Grandfather said, his eyes twinkling. "I have a suggestion. Let's take the van and go into town for breakfast!"

"I'll take the jeep," Larry said reluctantly. "Mr. and Mrs. Miller, why don't you ride with me? We'll meet at Minnie's Coffee Shoppe."

"Where's Betsy?" Jessie asked.

"My niece is horseback riding," Ralph said. "She'll be back soon, but I know she wouldn't care to join us."

Just then Betsy breezed in, her blonde curls tousled and her cheeks rosy.

"Betsy," Larry said, "how about breakfast in town with us?"

She hesitated, then lifted her chin. "No, thank you." She ran upstairs, but in a minute she rushed downstairs. "My room!" she shouted. "It's freezing in there!" She glared at Larry. "The window is smashed and there's broken glass all over."

"How did that happen?" Ralph asked.

"I have no idea," Betsy said, looking suspiciously at Larry. "Someone must have been trying to break into my room from the balcony."

"We'll pick up the glass and I'll buy a new pane in town," Larry said with a sigh.

"Poor Betsy," Violet said.

Betsy stared at Violet for a minute, as if she couldn't believe Violet would sympathize with her. Then, with a toss of her head, she went into the den.

Henry accompanied Larry upstairs and they swept up pieces of glass and fitted cardboard in the window.

On the way to Minnie's Coffee Shoppe, Benny said, "We'll have turkey for our big dinner, won't we?"

"We must have turkey for dinner," Davey said, a worried expression on his freckled face.

"We'll definitely have turkey!" Violet said, smiling at the two boys.

After a hearty breakfast of eggs, bacon, and toast, Ralph visited the barber shop, Grandfather went to buy a stove, Larry took Steven and Rose Miller to view a historic mansion, and the children bought groceries for lunch and dinner.

Afterward, Hannah and Davey went to meet their parents while the Aldens stopped at a drugstore for hot chocolate.

"I don't believe Betsy is guilty of all those mean things," Violet said. "Not after her window was broken."

Henry pushed his empty cup aside. "I'm not so sure."

"Why?" Jessie asked. "Betsy's window was broken. She wouldn't break it herself, would she?"

"Well, it's funny," Henry continued, leaning back in his chair. "If a burglar stood on the balcony and broke the window, most of the glass would be *inside* Betsy's bedroom. But we cleaned up most of the pieces *outside*, on the balcony."

"You mean that someone must have broken the glass from *inside* the house?" Jessie asked.

"Right," Henry answered. "Also, I didn't see any footprints on the balcony."

"I hope Betsy isn't doing bad things to Snowflake Inn," Soo Lee said, her dark eyes worried.

Jessie said, "Remember how Betsy glared at Larry? She must think he's the guilty one."

"Maybe he is," Violet said.

Henry, glancing at his watch, jumped up. "We're late. We have to meet Mr. Winston. Grandfather told me he'd meet us back at the inn."

When they arrived at the inn, Grandfather

was there with a big smile on his face. "Come into the kitchen," he said.

Curious, Benny rushed into the kitchen. "Wow!" he exclaimed.

Ralph Winston moved forward, running his hand over the surface of the new stove. "Why," he said in amazement, "this stove looks more like an antique than the one taken out of here." Clearly, he was pleased.

"It looks like an antique, but cooks and bakes like a modern stove." Grandfather chuckled. "You see, Ralph? You can modernize this inn and it won't lose its eighteenth-century character."

Ralph's mouth set in a stubborn line. "This stove is change enough! I don't want any more modern things to ruin Snowflake!"

"Why are you so obstinate, Dad?" Larry said, his voice rising. "Maybe you should give up the inn."

Jessie, sensing another argument, interrupted in a cheerful tone, "How about letting us cook lunch on the new stove?"

"Sounds great," said Grandfather.

That afternoon, the children each scooped

up a big bowl of fresh snow, then drizzled maple syrup over it for a treat. While eating the delicious sweet, they planned their holiday menu. Later, Larry drove the Aldens into town to buy groceries for the big feast.

After dinner, the children gathered around the piano in the den. Jessie played, and everyone, in loud, happy voices, sang "Over the River and Through the Woods."

Henry brought in an armful of firewood. Attempting to light the fire, though, he leaped up in dismay. "This wood!" he shouted angrily. "It's wet! It was fine this afternoon. I checked it!"

"You mean someone poured water over it?" Benny asked, frowning. "Just so we couldn't have a fire?"

"That's ridiculous!" Larry growled, throwing down a log in disgust. "No one would do that."

Violet's heart picked up a beat. Who was doing all these mean things? Was it Betsy? Or Larry? Why wouldn't they stop?

CHAPTER 11

Benny and the Secret Room

"So what if the firewood is wet!" Jessie exclaimed. "Who needs a fire?" She jumped up from the piano. "I have an idea. Let's bake holiday cookies!"

"Yes, yes," Benny responded. "We'll have a good time tonight."

"We can try out the new oven," Violet pointed out.

"Good idea," Henry said. "The oven needs testing before we roast the turkey tomorrow."

The children trooped into the kitchen,

bringing out cookie sheets and cookie cutters. Jessie preheated the oven.

Henry mixed sugar cookie dough, Violet rolled it out, and Davey and Benny cut out stars, bells, and candy canes.

Then Jessie mixed up dough for a batch of Russian tea balls. When her cookies were baked, Benny, Soo Lee, and Davey rolled them in powdered sugar. Next, they decorated some of the sugar cookies with red and green gum drops, others with sparkly candies.

The children topped the evening off by eating warm cookies and drinking cold milk. Bedtime arrived before they knew it.

Tucking himself in, Benny refused to think about all the bad things that had happened. Surely, nothing else bad would take place. Instead, he thought about the holiday feast the following evening. What fun it would be to cook the dinner. With happy thoughts of pumpkin pie and whipped cream, Benny drifted off to sleep.

In the morning the kitchen became a flurry of cooking activity as the children prepared the turkey, simmered the giblets, and boiled cranberries and sugar.

Rose Miller entered, surveying the busy kitchen. "May I give you a hand?"

"No, Mother," Hannah answered with a smile. "We've got everything under control."

"Well, all right," Rose said doubtfully. "But, please let me know if you need help." She backed out. "If you're sure you don't need me, your dad and I will go for a walk."

" 'Bye, Mom," Davey said, smiling and waving. "We'll be fine. The Aldens are showing us what to do."

Rose smiled, too. She seemed pleased that Hannah and Davey were helping in the kitchen and clearly enjoying themselves.

The Aldens turned back to their chores.

Davey and Soo Lee chopped onions for the stuffing. Benny diced celery. In a big bowl, Violet tore up pieces of bread, mixing in an egg, and Jessie simmered chicken broth to pour over it. Soo Lee sprinkled the mixture with salt, pepper, and sage. Hannah stirred the ingredients together. Next, Jessie and Benny stuffed the turkey cavity with the moist dressing.

Finally, Henry carried the roaster, with the twenty-pound turkey in it, to the oven and placed it inside.

"Hey, kids," Larry said, poking his head in, "let's take a sleigh ride down to the pond. You can help me feed the ducks and geese."

"Oh, boy!" Benny said. "Let's go."

"I thought most birds had flown south for the winter," Jessie said.

"These birds are on their way," Larry said with a chuckle, "but we can fill their stomachs so they'll have a good flight."

Violet thought it couldn't be Larry. He was too nice.

The sleigh ride reddened the children's cheeks and put big smiles on their faces.

When they arrived at the pond, a flock of geese had landed on the shore. Benny and Davey raced ahead, each with a bag of bird seed. After scattering the seed over the ground, the two boys were delighted to see the honking geese devour the food.

Violet and Henry, carrying seed, moved to another area where mallard ducks had settled.

Soo Lee fed a lone duck by an oak tree. Hannah and Jessie helped Larry unload a huge sack of feed and distribute it along the edge of the pond.

After the birds had been fed, the children climbed aboard the sleigh for the ride back to the inn.

"I hope nothing has happened to the turkey or cranberry sauce," Violet said. The way things had been going, she wasn't sure what they'd find next!

"Grandfather and Ralph will protect the kitchen," Jessie said reassuringly.

Overhearing these remarks, Benny jumped up and down on the bench. "Go faster, Larry!"

From an easy trot, Dobbin and Robin broke into a gallop and soon the children were back in the kitchen, pleased to find that everything was as they'd left it. They quickly prepared a late breakfast of cinnamon toast and oatmeal.

Davey rang the bell to announce that breakfast was ready, and everyone assembled around the dining-room table.

"We'd better not eat too much," Benny said. "We need to have a big appetite for our holiday dinner." Benny grinned at Betsy.

Betsy pushed aside the oatmeal. "I only wanted toast," she said.

Betsy's perfume tickled Benny's nose. He sneezed. "Ah-choo!"

Betsy rose and smiled suddenly. "I'll help you make the dinner. Then I'm going horse-back riding."

The children were all pleased with Betsy's offer of help and her good spirits.

After eating, the children and Betsy cleared the table, and set to work making biscuits, mashed potatoes, scalloped corn, candied yams, apple salad, and pumpkin pies.

Benny, who had been cutting up walnuts for the apple salad, sneezed again. "I'm going upstairs for a tissue," he said.

Jessie laughed. "Betsy's jasmine perfume makes you sneeze."

"I'm sorry," Betsy said. "I'll go riding now and you'll stop sneezing."

"I'll be back to help," Benny promised, hurrying to the steps.

On the way there, however, he slowed his steps, remembering the secret room. Maybe clues were hidden in there and he could be the one to find the mystery person. He was tired of the mean tricks.

Standing before the brick wall, Benny pushed one brick, then another, but the door didn't budge. At last, he pressed the right brick and the door swung open. Carefully, he inched forward. He'd only advanced a few steps, however, when the door clicked shut! Benny, his heart thudding, tried to see in the blackness. Now he was locked in the secret room and no one knew where he was! What should he do? Benny sank to the floor and put his head in his hands. What if he was in this dark, scary place forever?

CHAPTER 12

The Guilty One

Inside the secret room, Benny
wrinkled his nose, lifting his head. Jasmine!
Betsy's perfume followed him everywhere,
even here. Slowly, he moved about, unable
to see.

What if he missed the holiday feast? He
had to find a way out! His eyes were getting
used to the dark and he saw, on one wall, a
low, rounded door. When he twisted the
handle, the door opened. On hands and
knees, he emerged into the kitchen!

"Benny!" Violet called, pulling her

brother from under a worktable. "Where have you been?"

Henry leaned down, astonished. "Look how this wallpaper hides an opening in the wall. Where did you come from, Benny?"

"The secret room," Benny answered.

Jessie put her arm around his shoulders. "Poor Benny! You must have been scared."

"A little," he confessed in a low tone.

"Now we know how a person can get into Greta's locked kitchen," Henry said.

"And while I was in there I smelled *Betsy*'s perfume!" Benny said.

"Are you sure?" Soo Lee asked, dusting off a cobweb from Benny's shirt.

"Betsy must have been in there," Jessie said.

"But why would she creep around in that secret room?" Benny asked. "It's dark and scary."

"Well, if she was up to no good . . ." Henry began.

"And she didn't want anyone to know . . ." Violet added.

"I bet that's how she got into the locked kitchen to break the stove," Jessie said.

"What should we do?" Violet asked.

"Dinner's almost ready. I think we should wait until afterward before we do anything," Henry said.

"How are things going, children?" Grandfather said, as he came in just then. He sniffed. "Those pumpkin pies smell wonderful."

"We're right on schedule, Grandfather," Jessie said. "After we set the table, we'll take our baths and dress for dinner."

"Good, good," James Alden said. "I'm getting hungry."

"I *am* hungry!" Benny said.

Hannah smiled and turned to Violet. "I'm going to wear my new red dress," she said.

"I can't wait to see it," Violet answered, accompanying Hannah up the stairs.

Jessie and Henry followed.

Benny and Davey were last, staying behind to each dip a finger into the whipped cream for just a taste.

After the boys took their baths, they

slicked down their hair and pulled on their best sweaters.

The girls, already downstairs, were in the kitchen, dishing the food into bowls.

"Anything left for us to do?" Henry asked.

"Please take the turkey out of the oven," Jessie said. "Put it on the big platter, and set it at Grandfather's place for carving."

"Will do," answered Henry cheerfully.

"We're ready," Jessie pronounced, removing her apron.

Soo Lee rang the dinner bell.

When Steven and Rose Miller came in, Rose stepped back with a gasp. "How beautiful! How the crystal, silver, and china sparkle in the candlelight!"

Pleased, Henry smiled. All their hard work was appreciated. Down the center of the table bunches of holly, pine boughs, and pinecones surrounded six crimson candles. Clearly it was holiday time!

Grandfather sat at one end of the long table with the huge golden brown bird before him. At his left, Larry stared in amazement. "You kids have done a great job!" he marveled.

"I agree!" Ralph said, "I've never seen the dining room so festive and magnificent."

The smiling children stood in the doorway, admiring the table. Henry snapped a picture.

"Where's my niece?" Ralph asked, glancing about.

Soo Lee turned. But there was no Betsy!

Benny tugged on Jessie's sleeve, beckoning her to follow him. The other Aldens went along, too, trooping into the den.

Benny pointed to Betsy, who lay sobbing on the sofa.

"Betsy," Violet said, dashing forward and patting the young woman's shoulder. "What's wrong?"

Betsy continued to cry.

"What's wrong?" Benny repeated.

Betsy sat up. "It's all of you," she said between sobs.

Benny's eyes widened and he looked at Henry in bewilderment. Why was Betsy blaming them?

CHAPTER 13

Good-Bye, Snowflake Inn

"*Us?*" Jessie asked in disbelief. "What did *we* do?"

"Do? Why, you've been sweet and good to me," Betsy replied, "and I've repaid your kindness with meanness! I've done awful things! Things I'm ashamed of."

"You mean you released the horses?" Henry said.

Miserably, Betsy nodded.

"You stuffed up the chimney?" Davey asked.

Betsy nodded.

"You unplugged the refrigerator?" Soo Lee questioned.

Betsy nodded.

"You poured water over the firewood?" Violet said.

Betsy nodded.

"You broke the stove?" asked Benny.

Betsy nodded.

"You smashed your *own* window?" Jessie asked in surprise.

"Yes," Betsy whispered and hung her head. Tears trickled down her cheeks.

"Did you put the mouse in our room, too?" Violet asked.

"No! I didn't do that," Betsy said.

"Hey!" Ralph poked his head in. "What's the hold up?" When he saw Betsy, his smile became a frown. "What's wrong, dear?"

"Oh, Uncle Ralph, I must tell you something," Betsy murmured, wiping her eyes and blowing her nose. She rose.

Ralph, his face filled with concern, said, "What is it?"

Gently, Betsy guided her uncle into a big chair. Once he was sitting down, she confessed the awful things she'd done to the inn.

"But *why?*" Ralph asked.

"I wanted Larry to be blamed," she said between sniffles. "I thought if he were blamed, then I would inherit Snowflake Inn when you retired. I intended to sell it and open a restaurant in Philadelphia. I realize now how terrible I've been."

Uncle Ralph stood and put his arm around Betsy. "You've done some very bad things. But come into dinner, Betsy. We'll discuss this later."

When they arrived in the dining room, Grandfather was ready to carve the turkey.

The children sat down, relieved that, at last, the mystery had been solved.

Grandfather gave thanks for such a splendid dinner, then everyone heaped their plates with turkey, potatoes and gravy, dressing, cranberry sauce, corn, and candied yams.

"This is delicious," Steven Miller said.

"I peeled the potatoes," Davey piped up.

"And I baked these," Hannah said, passing a basket of biscuits.

"I'm proud of both of you," Rose said.

"Would you like to help me cook and bake when we get home?"

"Yes!" Davey and Hannah answered together.

After dinner, everyone helped clean up. Then the children sat in front of the kitchen fireplace.

"We're leaving at 5:30 in the morning," Hannah said. "I hate to go."

"We're sorry to see you go, too," Jessie said.

"I had a good time," Davey admitted, poking at the fire and watching the flames shoot up. "I didn't think I would."

"We both had fun," Hannah said. "I'm glad I came."

Henry said, "Davey, did you put a mouse in the girls' room?"

Davey looked guilty. "It was just a joke."

"It's all right, Davey," Jessie said. "We can take a joke."

Hannah turned to Violet. "Will you be my pen pal?"

"Oh, yes," Violet answered. "We'll write often!"

After they'd said good-bye, Jessie said, "I can't believe that I'd thought *they* were the troublemakers. They're really nice kids." The other Aldens agreed.

The next morning the Aldens rose early to pack and prepare breakfast. Hannah and Davey were already on their way back to Boston.

Betsy came into the kitchen. She poured a cup and sat at the kitchen table. "You know, Uncle Ralph forgave me! Everyone has been wonderful and I've been so rotten." She paused, sipping her coffee. "Uncle Ralph is going to help finance my restaurant, and I've promised to pay for all the damage I've caused."

"Was Larry angry?" Benny asked.

"Very angry," Larry said, coming in from the living room. "At first." He smiled at Betsy. "But I'm glad everything's out in the open and over, at last!"

"I hate myself for doing those things," Betsy said. "And you were so understanding."

"Hi, kids," Ralph said, entering the room. "Can you believe I'm hungry after our feast last night?"

Benny nodded. "I'm hungry, too."

"You know, Dad," Larry said, "I think you're right. Snowflake Inn is charming just the way it is."

Ralph winked. "We do need a phone, though. And a new boiler."

Chuckling, Larry gazed warmly at his father. "Do you think we've reached a compromise on our inn?"

"Guess so," Ralph answered. "If we each give a little, we'll have a mighty fine place."

After breakfast, the Aldens packed, then got in the car. As Grandfather pulled out of the drive, they all waved to Betsy, Larry, and Ralph, who stood in the doorway.

Grandfather gave a horn toot, and they were on their way back to Massachusetts!

It had been a great vacation, Jessie thought, leaning back on the seat. A vacation with a mystery. What could be better?

GERTRUDE CHANDLER WARNER discovered when she was teaching that many readers who like an exciting story could find no books that were both easy and fun to read. She decided to try to meet this need, and her first book, *The Boxcar Children*, quickly proved she had succeeded.

Miss Warner drew on her own experiences to write the mystery. As a child she spent hours watching trains go by on the tracks opposite her family home. She often dreamed about what it would be like to set up housekeeping in a caboose or freight car — the situation the Alden children find themselves in.

When Miss Warner received requests for more adventures involving Henry, Jessie, Violet, and Benny Alden, she began additional stories. In each, she chose a special setting and introduced unusual or eccentric characters who liked the unpredictable.

While the mystery element is central to each of Miss Warner's books, she never thought of them as strictly juvenile mysteries. She liked to stress the Aldens' independence and resourcefulness and their solid New England devotion to using up and making do. The Aldens go about most of their adventures with as little adult supervision as possible — something else that delights young readers.

Miss Warner lived in Putnam, Connecticut, until her death in 1979. During her lifetime, she received hundreds of letters from girls and boys telling her how much they liked her books.

The Mystery of the Snowy Day!

The Alden kids are trying to solve a really tough mystery. They have to figure out what to do when it's too wet and cold to play outdoors.

Of course, no mystery is ever too tough for the Boxcar Children. They solved this one right away! Just try the puzzles and activities on the next few pages. You'll have lots of fun — no matter what the weather!

The Puzzle Corner
Get out your pencils and solve these puzzles!

A New England Winter Wordsearch

New England is the northeasternmost part of the United States. It is made up of six states. The name of each state is hidden in this wordsearch. The names go up, down, backwards, diagonally, and sideways. Look for MAINE, NEW HAMPSHIRE, VERMONT, MASSACHUSETTS, RHODE ISLAND, CONNECTICUT.

```
N M N Q P M A Y B W D P M
V E R M O N T C O T N A A
L T W S N H E X T G A M S
A U O H T A W I N R L E S
T C E X A L C S O K S I A
B I M I L M A I N E I Y C
W T T E W O P V O O E O H
N C T O V R S S P J D Z U
S E N U R U E D H T O W S
B N Y S O E W E I I H N E
Y N I M T H C T H N R E T
S O Y P S O I V I M I E T
Z C G N O W L E N O T S S
```

All Boxed In

Snowflake Inn is filled with wonderful old furniture — some of it dates all the way back to the Revolutionary War. Even the stove in the kitchen is an antique!

This picture is all mixed up. To make it right, copy what you see in each box into the empty boxes below.

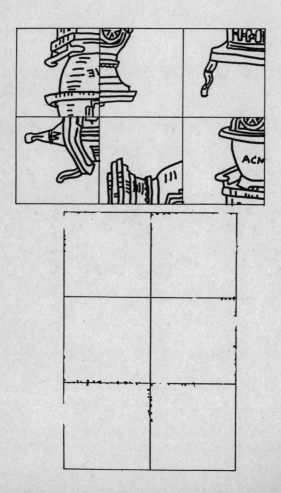

It's a Horse, of Course!

Ever since the Boxcar Children arrived, odd things have been going on at Snowflake Inn. Now, someone has let the horse out of the stable. The Alden kids are looking all over for him. But you won't have to search very hard — count by tens to connect the dots and you will find the horse.

Piece It Together

Oh, no! Someone has broken a window at the inn! Which of the pieces below will fix the window?

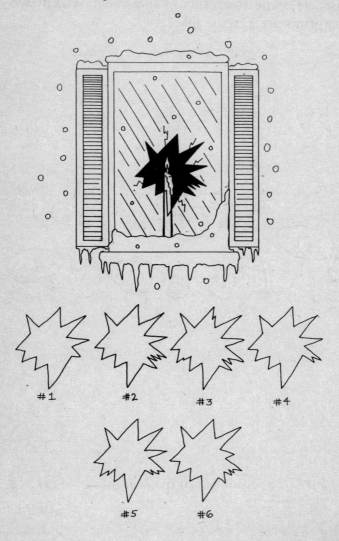

#1 #2 #3 #4

#5 #6

The Funny Footprints

Who has been causing all the trouble at the inn? While the Boxcar Children search for clues, they discover some footprints in the snow. Which two footprints are exactly alike?

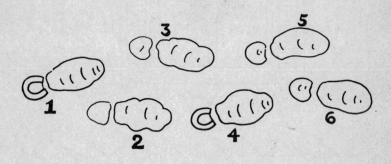

An Old-Fashioned Sing Along

Certain songs let you know the holidays are here. At this time of year, you're sure to hear "Jingle Bells" being sung with cheer. Why not sing along?

Jingle Bells

Dashing through the snow,
In a one-horse open sleigh,
O'er the fields we go,
Laughing all the way.
Bells on bob-tail ring,
Making spirits bright,
What fun it is to ride and sing
A sleighing song tonight.
Oh, Jingle Bells,
Jingle Bells,
Jingle all the way.
Oh, what fun
It is to ride,
In a one-horse open sleigh.

"Over the River and Through the Woods" is one of the Alden kids' favorite holiday songs. See if you can guess why!

Over the River and Through the Woods

Over the river and through the woods
To Grandfather's house we'll go.
The horse knows the way to carry the sleigh
Through the white and drifted snow.

Over the river and through the woods,
To Grandfather's house away!
We would not stop for a doll or top,
For tis Thanksgiving Day.

Over the river and through the woods,
When Grandmother sees us come,
She will say "Oh, dear, the children are here,
Bring a pie for everyone."
Over the river and through the woods,
Now Grandmother's cap I spy!
Hurrah for the fun!
Is the pudding done?
Hurrah for the pumpkin pie!

Thanks-for-the-Memories

The Boxcar Children will never forget the time they spent at Snowflake Inn. Color this picture. Try to remember everything you see. Then turn the page and take the memory test.

Circle the picture that is exactly the same as the one on page 109.

Yummy Treats to Make and Eat!

The Aldens love to cook. That's a good thing, because they also love to eat! Here are two of their favorite holiday recipes.

Deck the Halls Popcorn Balls

You will need:

5 tablespoons butter or margarine
3 cups miniature marshmallows
3 tablespoons powdered lime gelatin and powdered cherry or raspberry gelatin
3 quarts unsalted popcorn

Here's what you do:

1. Ask a grown-up to melt the butter in a saucepan.
2. Mix in the marshmallows.
3. Blend in the powdered lime gelatin.
4. Pour the whole mixture over the popcorn. Use your hands to make popcorn balls.
To make red popcorn balls, follow the same recipe using the cherry or raspberry powdered gelatin.

Maple Ice

You will need:

1 cup finely crushed ice
maple syrup
2 bowls

Here's what you do:

1. Divide the ice evenly between the two bowls.
2. Pour maple syrup over the ice in each bowl. Make sure all of the ice is covered in maple syrup.

Great Things to Make and Do!

The Boxcar Children are very creative. They can make great gifts from things you find around the house. Here are some of their best holiday gift-giving ideas!

The Happy Bird-Day Bird Feeder

Food is the best gift you can give the birds during the long, cold winter.

You will need:

1 large pinecone
1 piece of cord, 12 inches long
a spoon
peanut butter
birdseed

Here's what you do:

1. Tie the cord around the center of the pinecone.
2. Use a spoon to fill the pinecone with peanut butter.
3. Coat the peanut butter with birdseed.
4. Hang the feeder from a tree branch. The birds will fly right over for a tasty treat!

Let It Snow Paintings

A sparkly snow painting will melt anyone's heart.

You will need:

Tempera paint (in many colors)
construction paper or oaktag
a paintbrush
salt

Here's what you do:

1. Paint a picture using your paintbrush and paints.
2. Before the paint dries, sprinkle some salt over the parts of the painting you want to glisten. When the paint dries, your picture will sparkle wherever the salt has fallen.

A Boxcar Box!

No matter how great life is at Grandfather's house, the Alden children will always love the little red boxcar where they once lived. Here's how you can wrap your holiday gifts in their very own boxcar.

You will need:

a shoebox
tape
red wrapping paper
black construction paper
scissors
glue
a black marker

Here's what you do:

1. Place your gift inside the shoebox.
2. Tape the lid shut tight.
3. Wrap the shoebox in the red wrapping paper.
4. Cut four black circles from construction paper. These will be the wheels of the boxcar.
5. Glue the wheels to the front and the back of your boxcar.
6. Look at the little red boxcar on the front cover of this book. Use your marker to draw the lines that you see there.

Now your gift looks like a boxcar!

The Case of the Forgotten Present

Whose gift is this? These great gift tags will solve that mystery!

You will need:

1 sheet of oaktag
felt
markers
glitter
a pencil
scissors
glue
masking tape
newspaper

Here's what you do:

1. Decide what shape you would like your gift tag to be. Keep it simple—a star, a tree, a circle, or a rectangle all work well.
2. Use the pencil to draw your shape on the oaktag.
3. Cut the shape from the oaktag. This will be your stencil.
4. Tape the oaktag stencil to a piece of felt. Cut around the oaktag. You'll end up with a piece of felt the same shape as your stencil.
5. Remove the tape and the stencil from the felt.
6. Use your marker to write the name of the person who is receiving the gift onto the felt gift tag.
7. Place your gift tag on the newspaper.
8. Dab a little bit of glue onto the felt wherever you would like the glitter to stick.
9. Pour glitter onto your gift tag.
10. Lift up the gift tag and dump the extra glitter onto the newspaper.
11. When the glue is dry, tape or glue your gift tag to a wrapped gift.

Now you're sure to avoid the Great Gift Mix-Up!

Puzzle Answers
A New England Winter Wordsearch

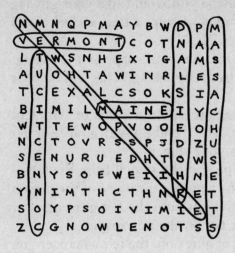

All Boxed In

It's a Horse, of Course!

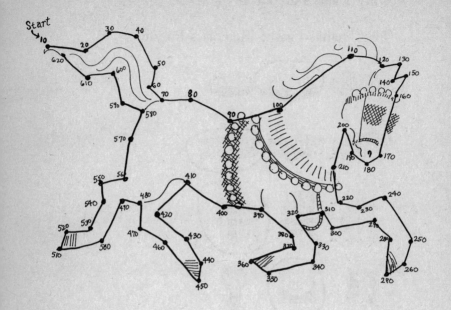

Piece It Together
Number 2 will fit.

The Funny Footprints
Only 1 and 4 are alike.

The Thanks-for-the-Memories Puzzle